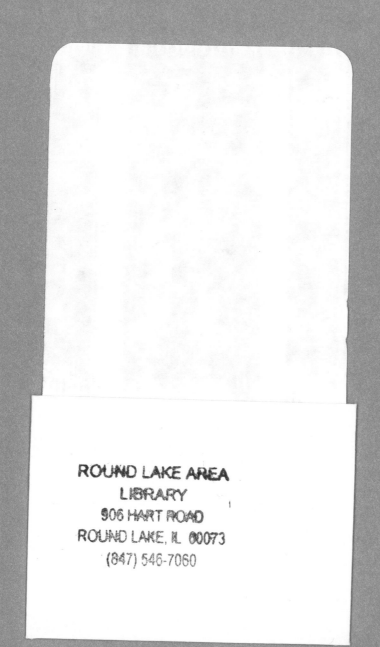

Which Witch is Which?

Which Witch is Which?

written by Judi Barrett

illustrated by
Sharleen Collicott

Atheneum Books for Young Readers
New York   London   Toronto   Sydney   Singapore

Atheneum Books for Young Readers
An imprint of Simon & Schuster Children's Publishing Division
1230 Avenue of the Americas
New York, New York 10020

Book design by Sonia Chaghatzbanian

The text of this book is set in Goudy.
The illustrations are rendered in gouache.

Printed in Hong Kong

2 4 6 8 10 9 7 5 3 1

Library of Congress Cataloging-in-Publication Data
Barrett, Judi.
Which witch is which? / by Judi Barrett ; illustrations by Sharleen Collicott.—1st ed.
p.   cm.
Summary: Rhyming text and illustrations present an assortment of witches in silly situations.
ISBN 0-689-82940-X
[1. Witches—Fiction. 2. Stories in rhyme.] I. Collicott, Sharleen, ill. II. Title.
PZ8.3.B25265 Wh 2001
[E]—dc21   99-011710

Which witch is trying to hitch?

Is it the one who is LEAN?

Is it the one who is green?

Is it the one who is **MEAN**?

Or is it the one who is clean?

Which witch has an awful itch?

Is it the one doing a jitterbug?

Is it the one lying on the rug?

Is it the one looking very smug?

Or is it the one playing with a pug?

Which witch is a sneaky snitch?

Is it the one looking glum?

Is it the one holding a plum?

Is it the one chewing gum?

Or is it the one playing a drum?

Which witch has an uncle named Mitch?

Is it the one petting a pig?

Is it the one doing a jig?

Is it the one holding a **twig**?

Or is it the one wearing a WIG?

Which witch looks radiantly rich?

Is it the one feeling **HoT**?

Is it the one stirring a pot ?

Is it the one eating an apricot?

Or is it the one tying a knot?

Which witch is about to pitch?

Is it the one with a **rash**?

Is it the one holding the trash?

Is it the one wearing a **sash**?

Or is it the one making a splash?

Which witch is learning to stitch?

Is it the one wearing socks?

Is it the one eating lox?

Is it the one looking in a box?

Or is it the one with chicken pox?

Which witch is flicking a switch?

Is it the one with a grin?

Is it the one with a twin?

Is it the one with a fin?

Or is it the one in a Spin?

Which witch is eating a sandwich?

Is it the one looking like a ghoul?

Is it the one acting like a FOOL?

Is it the one going to school?

Or is it the one sitting on a stool?

Which witch is causing a glitch?

Is it the one reading a book?

Is it the one dressed like a cook?

Is it the one hanging by a hook?

Or is it the one sitting in a nook?

Which witch is saying "Titch, titch"?

Is it the one with WILD HAIR?

Is it the one standing on a chair?

Is it the one talking to a bear?

Or is it the one drawing a square?

Which witch is eating spinach?

Is it the one looking like a KING?

Is it the one on a swing?

Is it the one wearing a ring?

Or is it the one about to sing?

Which witch fell in a ditch?

Is it the one riding on a broom?

Is it the one holding a balloon?

Is it the one looking at the *moon*?

Or is it the one eating a **prune**?